TIKTALA

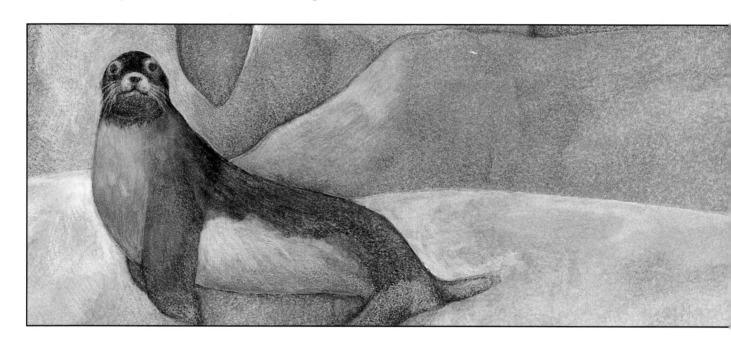

by Margaret Shaw~MacKinnon

paintings by László Gál

Holiday House / New York

Thank you to six pivotal helpers: the Manitoba Arts Council, Martha Brooks, George Swinton, Brian MacKinnon, Margaret E. Shaw and Kathryn Cole.

Text copyright © 1996 by Margaret Shaw-MacKinnon
Illustrations copyright © 1996 by László Gál
All rights reserved
Printed and bound in Hong Kong

First published in Canada by
Stoddart Publishing Co. Limited, Toronto

Library of Congress Cataloging-in-Publication Data
Shaw-MacKinnon, Margaret.
    Tiktala / Margaret Shaw-MacKinnon ; paintings by
László Gál.
        p.   cm.
    Summary: When the spirit guide changes her into a
seal, Tiktala learns the ways of seals and how harmful!
humans can be.
    ISBN 0-8234-1221-0 (alk. paper)
    1. Inuits—Juvenile fiction.   [1. Inuits—Fiction.
2. Eskimos—Fiction.   3. Seals (Animals)—Fiction.
4. Animals—Treatment—Fiction.]   I. Gál, László, ill.
II. Title.
PZ7.S53728Ti   1996   95-33198   CIP   AC
[Fic]—dc20

Printed and Bound in Hong Kong

To Dr. Edward Charles Shaw
and Margaret Elizabeth Shaw
for their love, intelligence, enthusiasm

To Brian, Margaret Eve, Arthur and Olivia

To the spirit who sent the dream
          — M. S.-M.

To Irene Aubrey
          — L.G.

In a village in the Far North, the soapstone carvers were worried. "We are forgetting our old ways," they said, and they called a meeting.

One girl, Tiktala, waited while her mother tried to coax her father to join them. Attatak sat in silence in front of the TV, shoulders slumped, eyes dim. He had barely spoken for days. Finally, Tiktala and her mother left without him.

The meeting was long and difficult. At last, Iguptak, the wisest woman in the village, spoke. "We have many skilled soapstone carvers who sell their work for high prices. But how many of our young people care about the animal spirits that enter the stones? Who among them is willing to learn the secrets of the old carvers?"

There was silence in the room.

"I am."

Everyone turned to see who had spoken.

"I am," Tiktala said again. Tiktala wasn't like her mother who believed in spirits, and she wasn't like her father who had lost his belief in everything. She had her own reasons for wanting to carve. She wanted to be famous and admired. She wanted money to buy things — a Walkman, a sewing machine, a snowmobile. Most of all, she wanted her father to notice her again. "I want to be a great carver."

"Be patient, Tiktala," one villager smiled. "Your time has not yet come."

But with her dark eyes Iguptak looked hard at Tiktala. "If you want to be a carver, you must go alone in search of a spirit helper. You must travel for three days towards the setting sun."

Tiktala was frightened, but she knew she must honor Iguptak's words. Her mother helped Tiktala prepare for the journey. When she said goodbye, Attatak raised his hand to wave, but never lifted his dark, bowed head.

For two long nights and three short days, Tiktala's feet crunched across the hardened snow. As the third night fell, she stopped, built a snow house and lit her lamp. It was the only light in the great expanse of darkness.

In the morning, when Tiktala awoke, she was amazed to find another shelter close by. The wind blew wispy snow ghosts around it. Tiktala called into the opening. At first the only sound was a raven's cry overhead. Then, out of the opening a strange voice spoke. It was old and young, and in between, male and female, and neither.

"You have reached the place of the spirit. What is your heart's desire?"

Tiktala shivered. "I . . . I want to be a great carver."

"Which animal do you most want to make?"

"The harp seal," Tiktala answered without thinking. "I mean — the polar bear! The bear is greater."

"Your first choice cannot be taken back. You must go all alone to a small island in the great ocean. Time will pass for you there, but it will not pass in your village. Agree to this if you still want to carve."

"I will go," said Tiktala. "But —"

Before she could ask how to get there, Tiktala found herself on a rocky island in a vast ice-filled ocean. She was lying on the ground and felt heavy and awkward. She looked down at what should have been her mittens and saw silver-grey fur, black claws — flippers. She tried to get away, but the flippers — her flippers — scratched and scrambled on the rock. Tiktala was a harp seal.

"Spirit!" Tiktala's cry rang out. "Change me back!" But no spirit answered.

Tiktala was sick with fear. She glanced up and froze, startled, for looking at her from the icy water's edge was a dark-eyed seal like herself.

"The spirit told me you were here," said the seal quietly. "I was chosen to help you make the journey north for summer fishing. Come."

"I can't," said Tiktala. "I'm human . . . I was human."

"I'll try to forgive you for that," replied the seal. "But I'll tell you right now, I've suffered at human hands. I'm angry that I was chosen to help you. I told the spirit you should go by yourself, but it wouldn't listen. There is no way out for either of us."

Tiktala looked out at the black, churning waters. She dreaded the sea, but she was more afraid of being left alone. She closed her eyes and heaved forward. "I am Tiktala!" she cried, as she entered the ocean.

"And I'm Tulimak, if you even care to know. Follow me."

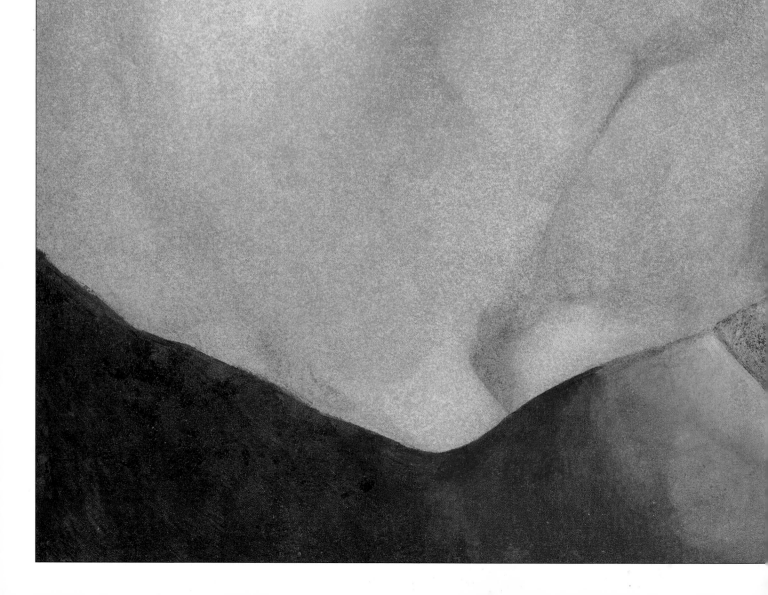

Tiktala felt a wave of panic as the rocky shore of the island sloped away into the shadowy depths. But when Tulimak shot downwards, Tiktala followed.

As they headed north, they passed over the blue peaks of an undersea mountain range. Tulimak dove into schools of silvery fish to catch and eat. Tiktala tried to keep up, but found herself stopping to peer through shafts of light at flowing curtains of fish in the strange undersea world. Eventually, Tulimak slowed down.

"You must eat, Tiktala," she ordered sharply, "or you will not have the energy to go on."

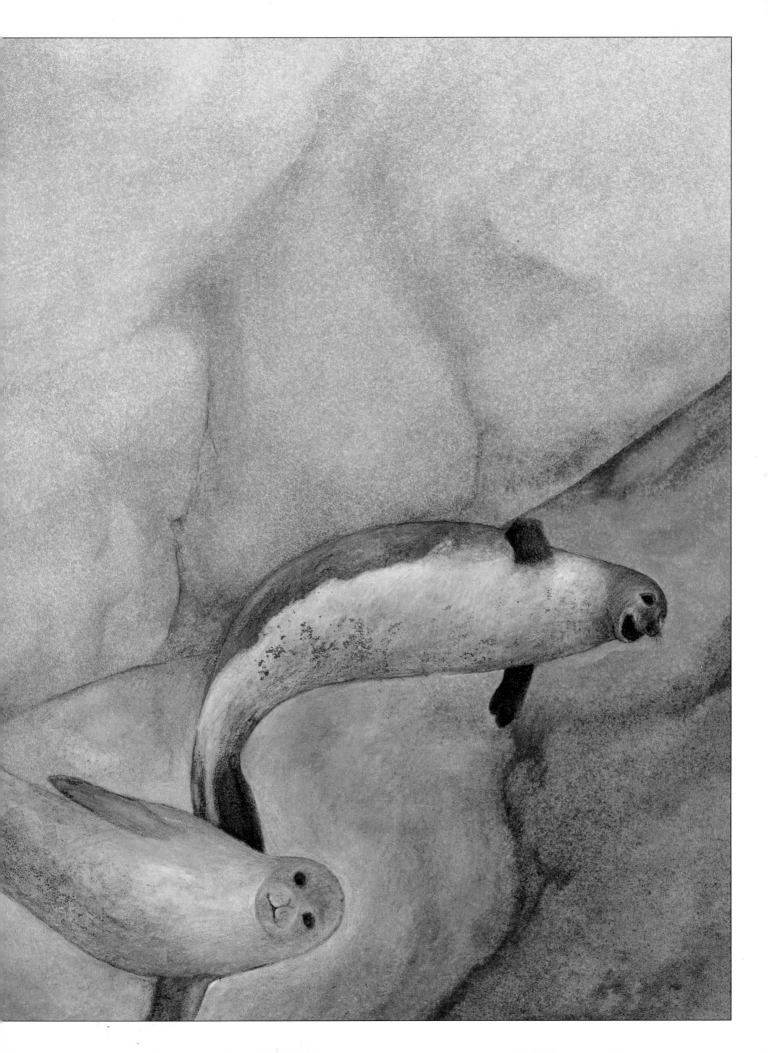

"Why do you hate me?" asked Tiktala. "I've never done anything to you."

"Your carver spirit told me you are like the people from the old tales, who would not take a seal's life unless the seal was ready to give it. But I know better." Tulimak's face was so sad. "You are human. Humans are cruel."

Tulimak swam off and began catching fish again. Very hungry, Tiktala tried to do the same, but she wasn't quick enough.

"I see I shall have to teach you everything," snapped Tulimak. "Look. There are some herring. Just speed into the school with your mouth open — and crunch, crunch!"

By evening, Tiktala and Tulimak had chased fish from the open sea into a coastal bay.

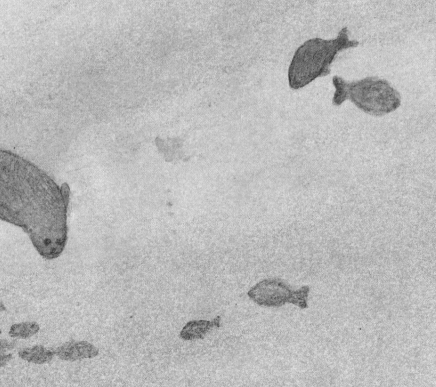

As the Northern Lights danced above them, Tiktala asked, "Where will we sleep?"

"Here," answered Tulimak, closing her eyes right there in the bay.

Tiktala was horrified. "But Tulimak, we must go ashore! Anything could get us here. How will we breathe?" In her panic, Tiktala reached out to touch Tulimak.

Tulimak opened one sleepy eye. "Don't worry, Tiktala, I am right beside you."

Tiktala stared into the vast, dim sea and imagined things flitting about in the shadows. Finally, unable to keep her eyes open any longer, she hung vertically in the water and slept. Inch by inch Tiktala sank, gently rocked in sea dreams, until it was time to breathe. Then still asleep, she floated up for air, and drifted downward again.

As Tiktala gained new skills on the journey, she began to enjoy Tulimak's world. And Tulimak began to accept Tiktala's company, often forgetting to be angry with her. Day after day, they swam, hunted, dozed — and sometimes even played.

Strong and graceful, with tremendous speed they traveled far, far north to the ice-filled sea, where all summer long the sun doesn't set. Such creatures they saw: huge walruses digging for clams, narwhals with their long, spiral tusks, birds diving for food, and many, many kinds of fish — cod, herring, capelin, Arctic char. After what seemed to be an endless string of days, Tiktala noticed Tulimak's shape was changing.

"We'll be going south next — to the pupping ground," Tulimak told her, the old sadness back in her voice. "I'll be having a pup in a few months time."

"You should have told me," Tiktala said.

"I'm sorry, Tiktala. You are no longer my enemy, but you were human once. Don't ask too much of me."

Tiktala looked away, all at once longing for her parents. "I've had sad things in my life, too."

A new chill entered the air. Overhead, Tiktala heard the flocks of geese, the terns and swans, all of them flying south. "Time to go," said Tulimak.

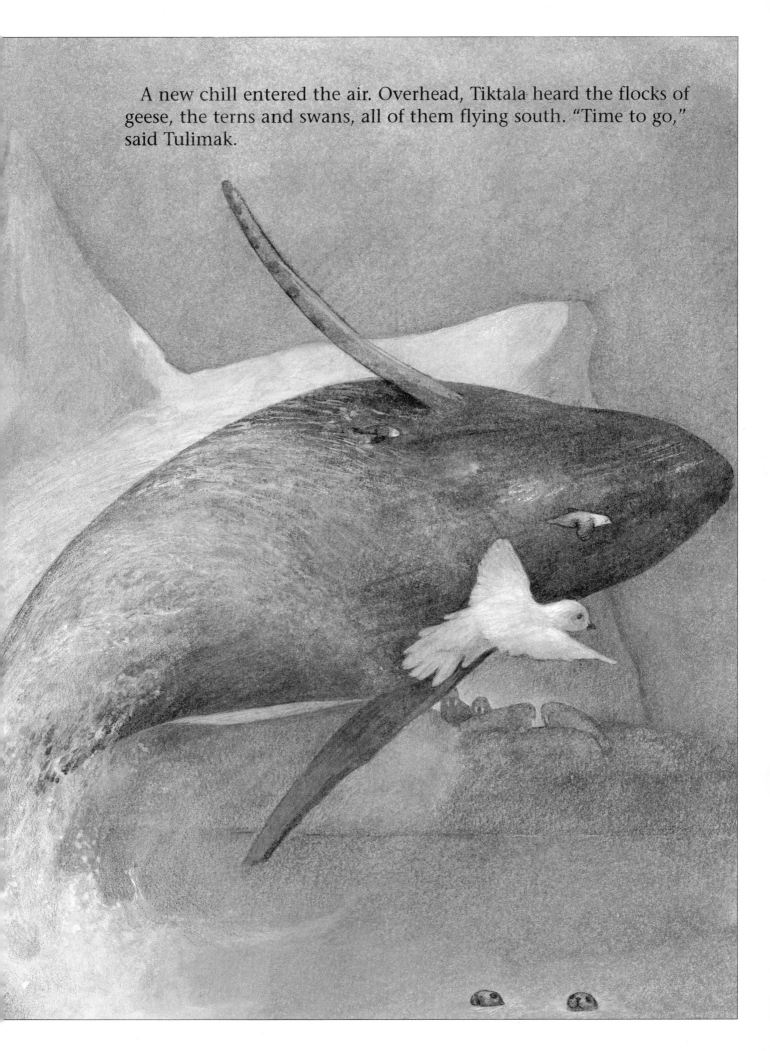

One day after journeying southward, Tiktala and Tulimak lay dozing on shore ice, when a polar bear with two hungry cubs spotted them. She signaled her cubs to stay put and loped towards the seals. Quite close, she lay on her belly and waited until she was sure they were sleeping. Then she began to creep forward, hidden by the whiteness of the snow. She was so intent on getting food for her cubs that she didn't notice the wind change direction. Tulimak's nostrils twitched and she woke instantly.

Polar bear! she thought. The water was nearby. There was time to save herself. Beside her Tiktala lay asleep. So *this* was why the spirit had chosen her to guide Tiktala. Revenge. She could let this bear snatch Tiktala's life away before she was ready to give it.

Suddenly, Tulimak spotted the dark nose of the bear rising over a hump of ice. She wavered an instant and then grabbed Tiktala's flipper. "Bear!"

Tulimak dove into the sea. Tiktala followed, with the bear close behind her. Its great claws ripped her hind flipper, but she managed to plunge into the water. With their hearts pounding, the two seals never slowed until they were a long way away. At last, Tulimak swam around to look at Tiktala's torn flipper. "I'm sorry you were hurt," she said, with real sorrow. Then, unexpectedly, she was filled with joy and a new sense of freedom. She swam up, up, up, breaking the surface, soaring through sunlight.

At last they reached the great meeting place in the south where thousands of seals gather on ice to have their pups. When the moment arrived, Tulimak struggled and her pup was born — tiny, glistening and new.

"I'd like you to name her," Tulimak told Tiktala.

Tiktala looked at the baby, a ball of soft, white fur lying there, and remembered how snow falls to earth in ever-new patterns of beauty. "I'll call her Aputi — snow on the ground," she said.

For the first time Tiktala truly yearned to be a soapstone carver. *That's what I'd carve,* she thought wistfully, *Tulimak and Aputi.*

Often, in the days that followed, Tiktala swam on her own, deep under the ice, while Tulimak fed Aputi. One morning when Tiktala came up, Tulimak was dozing alone. When Tiktala spotted Aputi, her heart almost stopped. A man was approaching her, talking softly, but holding a big wooden club in his hand. Awake now, Tulimak moaned in terror.

In that instant Tiktala knew. *This* was the human cruelty Tulimak had faced before. Aputi was not her first pup.

The man raised his weapon. Tiktala screamed and charged, desperate to place herself between the club and Aputi. As she reared up, the man disappeared and Tiktala, the girl, stood where he had been. Her arm was raised above her head, but instead of a club, she held a carving tool.

Aputi blinked up at her in surprise.

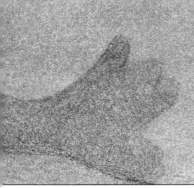

Tiktala knelt, dropping the tool on the snow. She gathered Aputi into her trembling arms and buried her face in the white, silky fur. Behind her, Tulimak barked softly in a language Tiktala no longer knew.

Tiktala stood on shaky legs and carried Aputi to her mother. She knelt and gently put her down. Aputi and Tulimak took one last look at her before slipping away, into the sea. Tiktala, tears streaming down her face, watched as the dark water closed over them.

"Now Tiktala," a voice within her said. The voice was old and young and in between, male and female and neither. "Now you can go home."

Tiktala found the carving tool she had dropped. She followed the bright beams of the rising sun over the purple-shadowed snow.

In three days she was home.